PROPHET'S END

BY SCOTT D. RUSSELL

Dorrance Publishing Co
585 Alpha Drive
Suite 103
Pittsburgh, PA 15238
Visit our website at *www.dorrancebookstore.com*

ISBN: 978-1-4809-4423-7
eISBN: 978-1-4809-4446-6

For Pete

For all First Responders, Police Officers, and Firefighters everywhere.

Hold fast to dreams
For if dreams die
Life is a broken-winged bird
That cannot fly
Hold fast to dreams
For when dreams go
Life is a barren field
Frozen with snow.

– Langston Hughes

ACKNOWLEDGMENTS

In the summer of 1984, I married a beautiful, partially deaf raven-haired girl named Margaret Jean DiSciullo. Without her, there would be no *Prophet's End* and, in fact, there would most likely be no me. Margaret, or "Peggy" as she is known to her family and friends, has been my savior. Peggy wedded a considerably flawed, emotionally wrecked, most likely suicidal maniac. That would be me. I have often pondered where I would be without her, or perhaps if I would exist at all. Peggy is also a breast cancer survivor.

I've done things in my life I am not proud of. There is no doubt I've hurt several people along the way, but some apologies are discounted, and I do not intend it to appear as if I am worthy of forgiveness. You see, I believe the moral of my volume is that one cannot change the future, and quite truthfully, neither can one alter the present.

The great majority of novels are prefaced with the fictitious disclaimer, "Any resemblance to real persons, living or dead is purely coincidental." So be it, however, in this case, this disclaimer would constitute a blatant lie. I suspect, however, that the publisher, if one actually deems this work suitable for public consumption, will place that very disclaimer in a prominent spot in this novella.

My closest friends in the world, other than my wife of course, hail originally from foreign countries. They are married to each other, a marriage made in heaven. They are Dr. Vladimir Privman and Dr. Violetta Thierbach. Vladimir, born in Uzbekistan, is a New York City endocrinologist. Vladimir, in his youth, was being trained by the Russian KGB. Violetta, a German born in Kazakhstan, has her own dental practice. Incredibly, I've only known them for less than two years. Also, implausibly, I met Vladimir directly owing to our mutual love of music. That is, our love of one particular artist, a young woman named Taimane Gardner, the Hawaiian-born daughter of a Samoan Princess. Taimane, a once in a lifetime artist, is a ukulele virtuoso. Imagine that!

I also wish to acknowledge my doctors, without whom I would not have acquired the strength to even begin this work. You see, I've suffered with Crohn's Disease for well over a decade, an insidious, incurable and anti-immune affliction that is becoming all too prevalent in today's world. Thanks to the wizardry of Dr. Josh Korzenik, a man who has also become a good friend, I am currently in a significant remission. Josh's RN, a young woman named Beth-Ann Norton, has also been a godsend. There are other great physicians as well, too numerous to list, as their names would take up lengthier space than the text of this book. Heartfelt thanks to all.

I would also like to acknowledge my friend, author and public servant Bill Hall, who has also been extremely helpful with his advice and expertise. Bill is an elected official, and in fact, a re-elected official, currently serving as County Commissioner in his home town in his native Oregon. Bill's fascinating book *McCallandia* is a not so far-fetched look at the past with a major dose of revisionist history. Bill Hall's book is a tome about the former Governor of Oregon, Tom McCall, and what could have been and even more so, what should have been.

Bill Hall has also been invaluable with suggestions, many of which that only a writer of his caliber could offer, most of which were implemented. His creativity is off the charts.

Pete Hamill is a hero of my tome. Therefore, the fictitious disclaimer would be of no use. It is my belief that all novels are at least, in small part, autobiographical, and *Prophet's End* is no exception. My character "Billy Farrell's" resemblance to yours truly is merely that he grew up (an achievement I've seldom been accused of accomplishing) in the neighborhood I describe as his. That is where the resemblance to Billy begins and ends. Billy is a noble character, I admittedly, am not.

Pete Hamill, as I stated, was an early hero of mine. Mr. Hamill remains an idol of mine, the explanation of which is prevalent throughout this book.

The character "Jennifer Swanson" is beyond a doubt, the heroine of this tale, and once more, the fictitious disclaimer is rendered entirely worthless. That is due to the fact there exists an impossibly beautiful young woman named Jennifer Bricker, and her resemblance to "Jennifer Swanson" is both intentional and the direct result of her inspiration and impact on my life. In truth, Jen Bricker has positively impacted the lives of countless people throughout the world, people of all nationalities, faiths and backgrounds. Jen Bricker, as is "Jen Swanson" in this book, is the embodiment of beauty and the selfless manifestation of hope and courage.

This tome, then, is all about hope. Without hope, we have nothing.

Prologue

In 1950s Bronx, New York, Billy Farrell is not an atypical youth. He isn't an atypical ten-year-old, that is, with the exception that Billy Farrell sees things others don't. You see, Billy Farrell can see the future. Not all of the future, mind you; however, glimpses of the future appear to him in dreams. These glimpses are random and they often do not have even a remote significance in Billy's own life.

It was a much simpler time during Billy's youth, a time when seemingly the greatest concern of American youngsters was how to avoid the dreaded Russians by squeezing oneself under a wooden school desk during practiced bomb shelter air raids. Paranoia over the threat of communism was rampant, and even more importantly, would the Brooklyn Dodgers ever defeat the New York Yankees in the World Series? Billy was a huge Dodgers fan and in the iconic season of 1955, that idea dominated his thoughts, other than his constant daydreaming regarding his little brunette classmate, Audrey Simmons. Would she ever notice him?

Billy Farrell, the son of Irish immigrants from Belfast, Northern Ireland, was a good student, not a great one, but his teachers loved him because he was considerate, thoughtful, and he tried hard to please. And he sure loved the Brooklyn Dodgers!

Billy was also an avid reader. It was that inclination that provided him with his first hero, a young aspiring columnist with the *New York Post*, a man who would go on to be recognized as one of the greatest journalists and authors in American history, Pete Hamill, himself the son of Irish immigrants from Belfast. Incredibly, Pete Hamill would become a close friend of Billy and under extraordinary circumstances.

Chapter One

Growing up here, you learned one bitter lesson: whenever something was destroyed for "the crime of being old, what replaced it was infinitely worse." – Pete Hamill

Billy Farrell was six years old when he first saw the girl in a dream. It was 1951, and Billy was in the first grade in elementary school at P.S. 61 in the South Bronx in New York City. She was approximately, Billy thought, his own age. She appeared as a visage one early morning as he was in that period between slumber and awakening. Her face was round and pretty, her eyes sparkled, and she seemed to smile. Billy seemed confused, he had never thought much about girls, but this one was different, he thought.

As for real girls, Billy's classmate in the first and second grade at P.S. 61 at 1550 Crotona Park East, was a pretty, slender girl named Audrey Simmons. Billy liked the way she laughed and the fact that she seemed very smart; however, Billy was shy, awkward, and a bit clumsy and Audrey paid him little or no attention. As luck would have it, several years later, Billy would attend Morris High School and would reunite with his classmate Audrey while both were freshmen in high school. Billy would sit behind Audrey in some of their classes and stare languidly at the back of her head. Although Billy had grown out of his awkwardness, he still remained quite shy with girls. However, his hormones were just beginning to kick in.

As Billy's adolescence progressed, the face of the young girl in his dreams would appear to him more frequently and as he grew, so did the visage. She appeared to age commensurately with Billy. By the time he was ten, Billy would often daydream about the girl he had never met and wondered why she consumed his dreams. By the time Billy was sixteen years old, he developed his initial crush on a girl who, he reasoned, did not even exist. Billy never spoke to anyone about his recurring dream for fear of being ridiculed.

The New York of Billy's childhood is no longer in existence. The South Bronx of his youth had large maple trees lining his neighborhood on Crotona Park East. Around the corner on Wilkins Avenue, there was a candy store, an ice cream parlor with wrought iron chairs with heart shaped backs and where a soda jerk would offer delicious egg creams, hot fudge and strawberry sundaes, root beer floats and malted milks and these delectable delights would be served in tall glasses. There was no graffiti on the walls.

In the Crotona Park of yesteryear, Billy would play with many of his young friends. There was Tony the Wop, Kevin the Mick, Lenny the Kike, and many others with nicknames which were not meant to demean, but to identify. It was an age before political correctness removed the alleged stigma of belonging to an ethnic group, as if it were derogatory. Everyone had each other's backs, so to speak, and no outsider was permitted to address Billy and his friends in such a manner. Lenny was a Kike, but he was "their kike," and so on. The names were administered, and each youngster considered it a badge of honor. It was a privilege to be accepted.

Billy and his younger brother, Evan, lived with their parents, Brian and Kathleen, in a tenement building at 1428 Crotona Park East in a third-floor apartment which overlooked Crotona Park. The huge maple trees which lined the street would provide shade for the elderly Jewish and Italian women who would congregate on the park benches facing the tenements. These women knew everyone and everything and gossiped freely about everyone in the area. They served as the eyes and ears of the community.

Billy's parents, Brian and Kathleen, were both immigrants from Belfast in Northern Ireland. Brian worked as a longshoreman and Kathleen a housewife. In the early 1950s, American paranoia over "**The Cold War**" even reached elementary school. Our government's preoccupation and fear of dreaded "communism" permeated our lives despite the fact that the great majority of the American public could not even define the word "communism." The irrational fears resulted in a truly dark era of the United States, "**The McCarthy Witch Hunt,**" a misguided investigation of those in politics and the entertainment industry, one headed by a previously obscure Senator named Joe McCarthy. His "**House Committee on Un-American Activities**" resulted in many innocent people losing their livelihoods and in some cases, their lives. Successful Hollywood careers were tarnished and ruined forever.

It was at the height of "**The Cold War**" that the absurd level of paranoia even managed to reach elementary schools, including Billy's P.S. 61 in the Bronx. Fearing a Russian atomic bomb attack, "Air Raid Drills" were initiated in public schools. Warning sirens sounded and students were instructed to dip beneath their wooden desks in a "duck and cover" maneuver. Billy and his classmates would crouch underneath their desks, facing away from the windows to protect against flying debris and glass. Then in 1953 Russia exploded its first hydrogen bomb. The Russians are coming! The Russians are coming! The illogical foolishness even reached major league baseball where the storied franchise the Cincinnati Reds changed their name to the Cincinnati Redlegs, not to be confused with the Chinese communists or the Russian "Reds."

Chapter Two

It was the year 1955 when Billy finally began to have dreams other than ones that revolved around the pretty girl with the dark hair and lovely round face. Billy loved baseball, and in particular, his beloved Brooklyn Dodgers. Billy's parents, Brian and Kathleen, were, of course, immigrants from Belfast in Northern Ireland, and although neither was interested in baseball, they encouraged their sons, Billy, ten, and his younger brother, Evan, eight, to pursue "American interests."

Billy watched the Dodgers on the family's twelve-inch black-and-white television in their third-floor Crotona Park East apartment. Billy was also permitted to listen to the Dodger games on his transistor radio as long as he had finished his homework. This was never a problem as Billy was an excellent student and one becoming increasingly interested in the art of writing.

The year 1955 was an iconic one for Billy's beloved Brooklyn Dodgers as they finally provided optimism to their faithful that they were capable of finally defeating their dreaded rivals, the New York Yankees, who seemed like perennial world champions. The Dodgers, although formidable in prior years, would seemingly always crumble when going head to head against the inhabitants of Yankee Stadium.

The classic World Series of 1955 came down to a winner take all seventh game and when Brian arrived home and surprised Billy with four tickets to the game at the historic Bronx venue. Billy was as thrilled as he had ever been during his brief lifetime. Kathleen, Billy's mom, reminded her husband that the game was during a school day. However, Brian responded, "The lad is a fine student.

I'm certain his teachers will understand." In fact, for the penultimate game six, the teachers had suspended class so that their students could hear the game on the radio.

Billy was so excited later that evening, that he could hardly sleep. It was approximately 1:00 A.M. when he finally drifted off, but for the initial time since he commenced dreaming, his dream was not of the pretty brunette with the round face, but of the historic seventh game of the World Series he was about to witness in person.

The vision in the dream was not crystal clear except for an amazing catch performed by a relatively obscure outfielder named Sandy Amoros. The vague details included Johnny Podres, the Dodgers young left-handed pitcher winning the game 2-0. Gil Hodges, Billy's favorite player on the Dodgers, would drive in both runs. However, the lucent vision which shocked Billy was that of an unlikely hero, a young Cuban outfielder named Edmundo Isasi "Sandy" Amoros. In Billy's vivid portion of the dream, Amoros, playing left field in the bottom of the sixth inning, would race to the left field corner, just a mere few feet from the foul pole and make a remarkable one handed catch, wheel and fire a strike to Dodger shortstop "Pee Wee" Reese, who in turn would throw a strike to Dodger first baseman Gil Hodges to complete a miraculous game saving double play. The image was indelible.

Billy awoke on that fateful day of October 4, 1955 with a sense of excitement and joy. Billy was both fascinated and confused in regard to his dream, which was both surrealistic and unimaginable. After all, he had never experienced a dream even remotely similar. Invariably, Billy's dreams revolved around the visage of the pretty little brunette girl with the round face, the girl who didn't even exist, he thought. Why would he suddenly experience a dream about the baseball game he was about to attend? Billy also reasoned that the final score in the dream, 2-0 in favor of the Dodgers, was extremely unlikely, since both the Yankees and Dodgers were renowned for their formidable offenses.

Billy rationalized he dreamed that Gil Hodges would drive in both runs because of the fact that Hodges was Billy's favorite player. He laughed when he thought of the absurdity of Amoros making an exceptional game saving catch. It wasn't as if Sandy Amoros wasn't a decent fielder, however, he was a rather obscure reserve player and in the projected lineups printed by the New York major dailies, Amoros wasn't even slated to start the game.

At 11:00 A.M., Brian and Kathleen gathered Billy and Evan and walked over to the IRT Subway station in order to head towards Yankee Stadium. Very few of the folks in that area had cars in those days. Upon switching to the Woodlawn Road train #4 at 149th Street, Billy's excitement grew as he anticipated seeing his heroes in their quest for the elusive World Series championship. The Brooklyn Dodgers had appeared in six prior World Series, but had never emerged victoriously. Billy fervently wished that his dream portended something wonderful was about to occur. Billy, of course, did not speak of his vision, not to his parents and not to his younger brother, Evan, who was more enthusiastic about the prospect of devouring ice cream and hot dogs than the game itself.

As the train entered the 161st Street and River Avenue subway stop, Billy's excitement reached fever pitch. The family walked purposefully to the gates, where Brian handed the ticket taker the four passes, and the Farrells were allowed passage into Yankee Stadium. Their seats were in grandstand Section One upstairs, behind home plate. After our National Anthem was played with the Yankees standing at their respective positions, Tommy Byrne, the veteran Yankees pitcher began his warm-ups. Billy suddenly recalled his dream of the night before. He remembered the vague part of the dream, the one where he saw his hero Gil Hodges knock in both runs in a complete game shutout by southpaw Johnny Podres. So, in the fourth inning when Hodges singled to drive in Roy Campanella giving the Dodgers a 1-0 lead, he cheered and smiled at the "coincidence."

Meanwhile, Johnny Podres was indeed pitching shutout ball, just as he had done in the dream. When Gil Hodges drove "Pee Wee" Reese home with a sacrifice fly in the top of the sixth inning, Billy cheered and also recalled the details of his dream. Billy thought to himself as Reese crossed home plate with the second run, that the probability of Amoros making a game saving catch was nil. After all, Amoros was not even in the game! However, when Dodger outfielder George "Shotgun" Shuba entered the game as a pinch-hitter for second baseman Don Zimmer shortly after Hodges's sacrifice fly, Billy's wheels began turning.

The move by Dodger manager, Walter Alston, would necessitate changes on defense. Therefore, when the Dodgers took the field to begin the bottom half of the sixth inning, Dodger left fielder Jim Gilliam switched to second base and Sandy Amoros entered the game as a defensive replacement in left field!

Billy immediately became animated, although he would still not inform his parents of his potentially being realized dream. Instead, he suddenly grabbed his father, Brian, by the hand and exclaimed, "C'mon, Dad!" Billy's dad reacted with some confusion, thinking that perhaps his son wanted to go to the restroom or the concessions stand, but what Billy wanted to do was to walk towards the left field grandstand in order to see Amoros's impending historical catch!

As Billy and his father stood upstairs near the left field foul pole, Brian asked his son, "What's this all about, lad?"

Billy replied, "You'll see, Dad."

When both Yankee stalwarts, Billy Martin and Gil McDougald, reached base to begin the inning, it appeared as if Dodger hurler Johnny Podres was on the ropes. There were runners on first and second and no one out. The next hitter was Yankee great "Yogi" Berra, who stood menacingly at the plate representing the lead run. When Berra sliced a long drive into the left field corner near the foul pole, the sold out crowd at Yankee Stadium held its collective breath. Sandy Amoros, the diminutive fleet footed Cuban, just inserted into the game for defensive purposes, seemingly came out of nowhere. Extending his right gloved hand while on the full gallop, he made a miraculous catch, spun and threw a strike to shortstop "Pee Wee" Reese, who in turn, fired a strike to Dodger first baseman Gil Hodges, who stretched for the throw which doubled Yankee base runner Gil McDougald off of first base. Double play! Exactly the sequence in Billy's dream!

The Dodgers went on and indeed, won the game 2-0 as Billy had also seen, but with less clarity. Upon returning to their seats behind home plate, Brian remarked to his wife, Kathleen.

"The lad apparently must have had a premonition. He took me to left field and we got to see the extraordinary catch. Pure luck!"

Billy was not about to tell his dad that the historic play was much more than pure luck.

CHAPTER THREE

In 1957, two years after the unusual, but foretelling "**Sandy Amoros Dream,**" Billy experienced another even more bizarre vision that was seemingly innocuous, but one that rendered the youngster confused and bewildered. As he lay in bed in the early morning hours, Billy grew restless. Suddenly, it was as if he was on a roller coaster and had entered some sort of wormhole. Intense and fleeting visions were coming at him at a frenetic pace. It was as if the boy had become entangled in some sort of time travel.

The youth began twitching and despite being asleep, his eyes opened wide and began rolling in his head. What began as a brief absurd image quickly evolved into some sort of surreal newsreel gone mad. First, he saw a rotund, bald man in a suit, seated at a table at which he was banging his shoe on at a place called the UN. The man seemed perturbed and he looked like someone's grandfather.

Following were a compendium of visions resembling highway signs being passed by a speeding vehicle, with the images arriving faster than the boy could manage to absorb them. He saw children and young adults all gyrating with hoops twirling around their hips and waists. He had a vision of four shaggy-haired mop-topped young men singing and performing on stage as young teenage girls went berserk and fainted.

Billy watched in a cacophony of silent and yet deafening sound, sort of a mute eloquence of absurdity. He saw a handsome, brown-skinned, superbly conditioned prize fighter standing over his fallen opponent, taunting him and mouthing the words, "Get up!"

The dizzying, delirious concoction of images seemed like ancient **hieroglyphics or Sanskrit** to the young boy. At once, he saw thousands of black people and white people, arm in arm, as they marched together with Washington's Capitol Building in the background. The people all appeared grim, but determined.

Several additional scenes flew by at an almost giddy pace. The decades were advancing at warp speed. At once, a new millennium had begun. Suddenly, there was an implosion and everything went black. The alarm clock had gone off.

As Billy grew a bit older, his recurrent dream, the one in which he merely saw the visage of the pretty brunette girl, increased in quantity. In the dreams, she never spoke. He just saw her attractive face, a face that appeared to continue to grow in age commensurately with his age. By 1961, Billy was sixteen years old and no longer as awkward or clumsy. However, Billy, still a bright student, was shy with the opposite sex; although a handsome youth, girls his age found him attractive. Billy's hormones were just about to kick in as he entered his freshman year at Morris High School in the South Bronx.

Morris High, at 166th Street and Boston Road, was noted for its impressive tower and was a terrific place for Billy to continue his formal education. Its alumni included "The King of Comedy" Milton Berle, famous dancer Arthur Murray, and Herman Joseph Muller, a Nobel Prize Winner in Medicine in the year 1946. Billy was at this point of his young life, a great student and a voracious reader. Therefore, he decided to attempt his hand at a career in journalism and joined the school newspaper, *The Tower*, which was both encouraged and recommended by his teachers.

Billy read newspapers ravenously, and in the New York of 1961, there were a multitude of major dailies, and being from a liberal household as both his mom, Kathleen and dad, Brian, being sensitive to injustice, something they were both subjected to in their youth in Northern Ireland, Billy's favorite newspaper was the renowned left-leaning *New York Post*.

The Editor-in-Chief at the *Post* was a crusty middle-aged, hard-drinking, chain-smoking tousled haired man named James Wechsler, who was a renowned fighter for civil rights, labor, and the underdog in general. Billy's dad would read the *Post* religiously and discuss world events with his eager son. In particular, young Billy had developed an affinity for a young writer at the *Post*, a twenty-six-year-old aspiring journalist named Pete Hamill. Hamill at the time toiled as a beat writer who covered murders and fires, but penned an occasional column. Billy loved the manner in which Hamill strung words together as did

Billy's dad, Brian. Brian referred to the young journalist as a "wordsmith." Hamill, Billy felt, wrote about New York City and its inhabitants with a grace, style, and flair which seemed beyond imagination. Billy loved Hamill's passion and his utter disdain for injustice, blowhards and phonies. Upon seeing his father bring home the evening edition of the *Post* each night, Billy would anxiously flip through the pages in hope of finding an event or occurrence that Hamill covered. Upon finding something written by Pete Hamill, Billy would never be disappointed.

As a freshman in high school, Billy was pleased upon seeing that Audrey Simmons, his elementary school classmate, was once more in several of his classes. He had not seen her for several years and now she appeared even more attractive to him, since he was quickly growing into manhood and Audrey into womanhood. This time, however, Audrey, who never paid much attention to the younger, awkward Billy Farrell, was attracted to the now handsome and intelligent young man. Billy, although still quite shy, was surprised when Audrey caught him peering at her and smiled at him. It gave him a funny feeling he was not familiar with, a good feeling.

Meanwhile, as the school year progressed, Billy's dreams of the mysterious girl with the round face were becoming more frequent. Her visage now haunted his waking hours as well, as he frequently daydreamed about her, wondering who she was and why she possessed his thoughts, and with his hormones kicking in, he found her alluring. As alluring, that is, as a young lady can be to a teenager lacking in maturity.

Something else began to occur during Billy's sleeping hours; for the first time since 1955 when he dreamed in advance of the Brooklyn Dodgers World Series victory, he began to experience visions of the future, other than the weird "newsreel dream" he briefly endured. It began oddly enough with another baseball incident, this despite the fact that Billy's interest in baseball had waned. His beloved Dodgers had departed for Los Angeles in 1958, and that plus the fact that he now enjoyed other arts and endeavors lessened his love for the game of baseball. Therefore, he thought it strange when he experienced a vivid dream that involved a team and a player he wasn't even following.

On the evening of Monday May 8, 1961, Billy, now sixteen years of age, completed his homework, made sure to read the *New York Times* and as was his wont, the *New York Post*, and went to bed. He was about to have that unforeseen dream. As he lay in the darkness, Billy began to see images of a baseball game, a game at a place called Metropolitan Stadium in Minneapolis. Distinctly, he envisioned this tall strapping left handed hitter step up to the plate and he saw the name "Jim Gentile" listed in block letters below his image. Gentile was wearing a Baltimore Orioles uniform. Billy noticed that the bases were loaded and it was the top of the first inning.

Although not even remotely interested in the game, he watched as a Minnesota Twin pitcher delivered a pitch which Gentile immediately blasted over the fence for a grand slam home run, a rare feat by itself. As the dream continued, he once more saw Jim Gentile step to the plate with the bases loaded. Was this a dream replay? Billy soon noticed that it was not and that the game had entered the second inning. Once more, Jim Gentile swung the bat and hit still another grand slam home run! Back to back grand slam home runs on successive pitches, as well. When Billy awoke that morning, his odd dream remained vivid in his mind.

Billy entered the kitchen for breakfast and found the morning edition of the *New York Daily News* where his father had left it on the kitchen table. He turned to the sports section and read that evening's pitching probable pitchers. He immediately saw that the Baltimore Orioles were indeed, playing the Minnesota Twins at Metropolitan Stadium in Baltimore later that evening. He suddenly thought back to his prophetic dream of six years earlier, when Sandy Amoros had made his now memorable catch in game seven of the iconic World Series in 1955.

Still hesitant to inform anyone of his questionable gift, if that's indeed, what it was, Billy pondered if he should inform someone regarding the possibility that he had somehow unwittingly and unknowingly acquired some form of clairvoyance. Therefore, he went to school that day, but, following class, he told his mom that he'd be late that afternoon. Billy, now sixteen years of age and trustworthy and mature, took the IRT Subway down to Manhattan. He hoped to meet his idol, the columnist and writer for the *New York Post*, Pete Hamill.

As Billy rode the subway to his destination, he had absolutely no idea what he was going to say to Pete Hamill if he actually met him; however, he was compelled to at least try.

Chapter Four

As Billy emerged from the subway in the heart of Manhattan, he was awe struck by the size of the buildings and the thousands of people scurrying in every conceivable direction, all seemingly with a sense of purpose. It wasn't as if the boy was experiencing his initial trip to the Big Apple, since his parents had taken him to Radio City Music Hall, Carnegie Hall, and Madison Square Garden, however, this was indeed, his first excursion alone. The youngster, although slightly overwhelmed by the vast city, suddenly recalled his own goal as he approached the offices of the *New York Post*, the headquarters of his idol, journalist Pete Hamill.

Billy entered the offices of the *New York Post* and the somewhat shy sixteen year-old asked a pleasant and attractive young receptionist if Mr. Hamill was in. The young lady paused, stared at the polite youngster and asked quizzically, "Do you have an appointment with Mr. Hamill?"

"No ma'am, but I'd only take a few moments."

The young woman, responded, "Well, I think you may be in luck. This is one of the occasions that Pete is in the office. Just go down this hallway and turn left. I believe you'll find him in the second room on the right."

"Thank you, ma'am."

"Aren't you polite?!" she exclaimed and smiled at the attractive youngster.

Pete Hamill sat at a chair overlooking the street below and he and the Editor-in-Chief, James Wechsler, were deep in conversation.

Wechsler had a cigarette in his hand and his ashtray was overflowing with cigarette butts. Wechsler sported shirt sleeves and a bow-tie and appeared slightly disheveled. Wechsler seemed a bit perturbed.

"Dorothy doesn't want me speaking to Doyle that way. How else am I going to get his ass to provide the information we need? Screw her!"

Dorothy Schiff was the Publisher of the *N.Y. Post*.

Pete Hamill responded, "Frank Doyle is the Press Secretary for the entire New York City Police Department. Hell, wasn't he a reporter for the *N.Y. Daily Mirror*?"

"Yeah, Pete, but sometimes I think he forgot about us peons. I'll just have to exercise more tact."

Suddenly, both James Wechsler and Pete Hamill became aware of the youngster standing in their doorway with a look of astonishment and awe on his face. Pete Hamill was the first to speak.

"Can I help you, young man?" Billy gulped before replying.

"You're Pete Hamill! I mean Mr. Hamill."

"The last time I checked, I was. And with whom do I have the pleasure of speaking?"

"I'm Billy. I'm a student at Morris High School in the Bronx and I write for our school newspaper and I think you're great!"

"How old are you, Billy?"

"I'm sixteen."

James Wechsler responded to the telephone ringing. "It's Dorothy! I'll see you later."

With that, Wechsler arose from his seat and as he left the room, he turned to Billy. "Nice meeting you, young man. When you graduate, perhaps we can use a cub reporter."

Pete Hamill then spoke. "Thanks for the compliment, Billy. You made my day."

"I love the way you write about the city, Mr. Hamill."

"It's Pete, not 'Mr.,' Billy."

Pete Hamill paused before continuing.

"So, what brings you here, Billy?"

"I have these dreams, really weird dreams. I see things in the future."

"Can you give me an example, Billy?"

"When I was ten, in 1955, I dreamed the Dodgers would win the World Series. I dreamed of Sandy Amoros's catch the night before it happened."

Pete Hamill peered at young Billy and appeared skeptical although Billy did not pick up on his incredulity. Pete liked Billy, however, now realized that he was no doubt dealing with someone either delusional or putting him on.

"Oh? That was a helluva catch! Without Sandy's play, the Dodgers most likely would have lost that game and it would still be 'wait until next year'."

Pete laughed and hesitated before continuing.

"Can you tell me what the lottery numbers will be tonight, Billy?"

"My dreams are random, I'm afraid, sir. I keep dreaming about a pretty girl with dark hair and a round face, but I don't think she even exists."

Pete Hamill laughed once more before responding. "Ha! I've had a few dreams about girls like that, too!"

Billy appeared briefly confused, but composed himself to speak.

"It's not like that, Mr., I mean Pete, all I see is this girl's face. I've never met her."

Pete leaned back in his chair before replying. "Have you had any other dreams recently, Billy?"

"Yes, sir, Pete, I had a vivid dream last night. I saw a guy hit two grand slam home runs in back to back at bats in the first and second inning."

Pete smiled and replied. He was humoring the boy.

"Was it Mickey Mantle?"

"No, actually it was Jim Gentile."

"Jim Gentile of the Baltimore Orioles?"

"Yes, Jim Gentile of the Orioles. And he's going to hit them tonight."

Pete paused and picked the morning paper off of his desk. He flipped to the sports section and read that Baltimore was in Minnesota to play the Twins.

"Back to back home runs in successive innings, huh, Billy? That would be quite a feat."

Billy, of course, did not realize that Pete Hamill was toying with him. "Yes, Pete, and on successive pitches."

"That's even more impressive, son."

At that point, James Wechsler returned and stood in the doorway.

"Pete, Dorothy wants us both in her office. She's got Doyle on the horn and he's livid."

Pete arose from his seat and grasped Billy's hand and spoke. "Sorry, but I have to go. Nice meeting you!"

Billy thanked his hero and walked out of the office, but not before getting Pete to sign an edition of that evening's *New York Post*.

CHAPTER FIVE

On the morning of Wednesday, May 10, 1961, Billy awoke and sleepily sauntered to the kitchen where Brian, his dad, was having breakfast and reading the morning edition of the *Daily News*. Billy was actually half-hoping that his dream did not bear fruition, these visions were beginning to frighten him, all that is, except the recurrent vision of the pretty brunette girl with the round face.

"Can I see the sports section, Dad?"

"Of course, you can, lad. Didja see what that Baltimore hitter accomplished last night in Minnesota, son?"

"Was it Jim Gentile, dad?"

"How didja know, lad? You must've been listening to your transistor radio while in bed last evening. Don't worry, I won't tell your mom."

Billy glanced briefly at the headline in the sports section which read,

Gentile Blasts Two Grand Slam Homers in Historic Feat

Billy did not even have to read the article to know they came in the initial two innings of the game. As he prepared for his school day, Billy paused while brushing his teeth and stared into the mirror. He wondered exactly who the sixteen-year-old peering back at him really was. Why me? Why was I chosen to receive these foretelling dreams? What force allowed him to foresee these events? Will these visions persist or was the Amoros catch and Jim Gentile's historic feat just periodic glimpses into the future?

Billy also pondered whether or not he should tell anyone of his gift, if that's what it was. Would they question his sanity? Would they suggest psychiatric observation? And what about the pretty little brunette girl, as her visage was becoming even more prevalent during the hours he slept. Billy was actually becoming slightly aroused by her "presence," although all he saw was her face. Was I losing my mind? Am I possessed by some demon?

At school that day, Billy's concentration waned. He was extremely hesitant about the prospect of informing anyone about his predicament, if it indeed, was actually a dilemma. Then suddenly he recalled meeting his idol, Pete Hamill, the previous afternoon.

Chapter Six

Pete Hamill, bleary eyed, rushed into the offices of the *New York Post*. James Wechsler was seated at his desk, smoking a cigarette and typing furiously. He seemed possessed and was slightly startled when Hamill interrupted him breathlessly.

"Billy, the boy who was here yesterday, do you recall his name?"

"Yeah, you just said it, it's Billy."

Hamill laughed at Wechsler's intentional wiseass response before continuing.

"I know that, Jimmy. I mean did he offer his last name?"

"Not that I recall. I seem to remember he said he wrote for his high school paper in the Bronx. Was it Roosevelt High, Monroe High, or Samuel Gompers?"

Wechsler took a deep drag on his cigarette and responded.

"Perhaps Morris High?"

Pete snapped his fingers.

"Yeah, I think that's it! I've got to find him!"

"What's this all about, Pete?"

"I'm not sure, Jimmy. This kid may have some real special gifts. He sees things"

James Wechsler chuckled.

"Hell, I see things, too. I just saw something this morning that I wish to God that I could unsee!

"What was so ghastly, Jimmy?"

"I just saw Erma Bombeck** wearing shorts!" Hamill laughed uproariously before replying. "Jesus, I just ate! That is some disturbing imagery."

"Hey, Pete, if the kid is truly gifted, tell him he can intern here this summer."

"Sure, Jimmy."

Pete Hamill was not certain that he should inform his boss and friend of Billy's gifts. He had a hunch that the youngster may endanger himself. Hamill made a mental note to call Morris High School in order to learn which students wrote for the school paper. He knew that correctly forecasting Jim Gentile's historic feat was not some sort of accidental chance. Something truly bizarre was afoot.[1]

---

[1] Erma Bombeck was a heavyset humorist and syndicated columnist.

Chapter Seven

Upon calling Morris High School, Pete was informed that there were three youngsters named William contributing to the school's newspaper, *The Tower*. Pete planned to visit Morris High that Friday in order to seek out the seemingly clairvoyant Billy. He wouldn't have to.

Later that afternoon, Pete Hamill sat alone in his office. He had just returned from a meeting with Mayor Wagner at Gracie Mansion, the official residence of the Mayor of New York, Robert F. Wagner, when he looked up from his desk and saw Billy, once more standing outside the doorway of his office.

Before Pete could even greet his unexpected visitor, the boy spoke.

"I'm scared, Pete. I'm really scared."

Pete Hamill arose from his chair, walked over to Billy and put his arm around him. He closed the door to his office.

"I can understand, son. Have you shared this gift with anyone other than me, Billy?"

"No sir, I haven't. You're the only person I've told about it."

"Not even your parents?"

"No sir, not even them. I love them, but I don't want them thinking I'm crazy."

"You mentioned knowing about the Amoros catch? You never told anyone about that?"

"No sir, I was only ten."

Billy paused briefly before continuing.

"I'm really scared, Pete. Why is this happening to me? Why me? Why was I chosen and by whom was I chosen?"

Pete stared out of the window onto the streets of Gotham, deep in thought.

"Billy, you've got my word. I'll never tell anyone. If you have any other dreams or visions, please know that you can trust me. I'm not sure that it would be wise to allow anyone to know that on occasion you have these visions that all seem to be realized."

Pete reached for a pen on his desk and began scribbling a note. "Billy, this is my home telephone. Not too many folks know it. Call me at any time. I mean it."

"You don't know how much I appreciate that, Pete."

"Tell me, Billy, you mentioned this recurring dream or vision about a young girl. What's your gut feeling? Do you think she really exists? I mean, Sandy Amoros and Jim Gentile certainly exist!"

"Gee, I don't know, sir. All I do know is that she's real pretty and that she makes me feel funny, if you know what I mean. But I can only see her face."

"Billy, does she ever speak in your dreams?"

"No sir, she's silent and there's one more thing. I began seeing her when I was six, but she's grown as I have. She seems to get older as I do. She looks about sixteen, my age."

Pete walked over to the window, seemingly deep in thought.

"I've got an idea, Billy. Can you describe her? You know, can you describe her facial features and complexion? You're a writer, I suspect that you can."

"I can give it a try, Pete. Let's see, she's got dark hair."

Pete interrupted Billy. "No, don't describe her to me. I'm going to bring in a sketch artist from the New York Police Department. He's a good friend of mine. You won't have to tell him why he's drawing her."

"Sure, Pete, I can do that. He works for the Police Department? I've often thought that one day I can become a police officer or a writer, Mr. Hamill."

Pete Hamill laughed before responding.

"I knew I liked you, Billy! Wow, two thankless jobs, not one! By the way, Billy, what's your full name?"

"It's William Fitzgerald Farrell, sir. My parents are from Belfast in Northern Ireland."

"Are you kidding me, Billy? My parents are also from Belfast!"

"I'm aware of that, Pete. You wrote about them in one of your columns."

"Wow, you really do read my work!"

"When should I come in to meet the sketch artist, Pete?"

"I'm having lunch with him tomorrow. Can you get here after school?"

"I sure can, I'm looking forward to solving this mystery."

"You're not the only one, that is, Billy."

Chapter Eight

Ed Barrow, the slender middle-aged African American sketch artist for the NYPD, smiled at Billy as he sat in Pete Hamill's office at the *New York Post*. He had just completed the drawing of the young round faced beauty of Billy's dreams. Ed Barrow spoke.

"I wish more of the people I dealt with were as descriptive as you are, Billy. I believe you've got a great future in communications. So, how did we do?"

"You've really captured exactly the way she looks, Mr. Barrow. Wow, you can really draw!"

"Who is she, Billy? Is she missing?"

"I'm not exactly sure who she is, sir. I just saw her a few times."

Billy hesitated before continuing.

"I'm not even sure if she exists."

Ed Barrow laughed before responding.

"Well, I hope you find out she's real, Billy. She's really pretty, whoever she is!"

Pete Hamill arose from his chair and shook Ed Barrow's hand before replying.

"Thanks again, Ed. Will I see you at ringside for the Denny Moyer fight at the Garden this Friday?"

"If I can escape from the wife, I'll be there, Pete. Say, who is this girl I just drew, anyhow?"

Pete Hamill winked at Barrow and answered, "Damned if I know!"

Chapter Nine

In the year 1963, as the burgeoning career of twenty-eight-year-old Pete Hamill ascended to new heights, eighteen-year-old Billy's horizons also expanded as he was rapidly growing out of his awkwardness and the intelligent, handsome youth was quickly evolving into a young man. However, during the year, Pete Hamill was in the midst of a major career change, one that would relocate him to Europe to begin anew as a contributing editor to ***The Saturday Evening Post***.

Despite the fact that Billy was flourishing as a young man, he continued to have dreams and visions of the beautiful dark-haired girl with the round face, and as he had experienced before, she continued to seem to grow commensurately in age with him. However, she still remained silent in the dreams and only appeared as a visage. Hamill would call from Europe on occasion, but the differences in time zones and their lives precluded a closer relationship.

Billy, now a senior at Morris High, had begun to date the girl he had earlier had a crush on, Audrey Simmons, his classmate, but then Billy had a life-altering dream. Audrey was enamored with Billy and he, in turn, found her extremely attractive; however, his dream suddenly and entirely forever revised his relationship with Audrey.

One evening in early spring, only weeks before he was to take Audrey to the senior prom, Billy had a vivid dream about the beautiful girl with the round face. In the vision, Billy saw himself in a church, surrounded by friends and family seated in pews. He stood in front of the altar and turned to see a young woman seated, not standing, next to him. She wore a beautiful white wedding dress and a veil. In the dream, he lifted the veil and there sat the beautiful girl with the dark hair, the girl he had constantly dreamed about! He was about to marry her!

Billy's dreams to that point invariably bore fruition without exception. Therefore, he knew in his heart and mind that he would someday marry this girl despite the fact that he had no idea who she was. He also knew that not only was this the girl of his dreams, but that she was **LITERALLY** that.

In early June of 1961, Billy had what he thought an absurd vision. He dreamed that a baseball player named Roger Maris would hit a historic home run on October 1st against a pitcher he had never heard of, Tracy Stallard. If that wasn't ridiculous enough, in the dream, the ball would be caught by a truck driver from Brooklyn named Sal Durante. He had informed Pete Hamill of this vision, and although they both shared a great laugh, both Hamill and Billy were certain the event would take place, and when it did, all Hamill could do was to shake his head and laugh uproariously and lament the fact that Las Vegas provided no odds for predicting that sort of outcome.

Meanwhile, before the dream of his impending wedding, Audrey Simmons, Billy's senior prom date and girlfriend, frequently spoke to Billy about someday being wed to him. After all, she considered them high school sweethearts and she was smitten with him.

Billy, of course, had never confided any of his dreams to anyone other than Pete Hamill, his mentor and friend. Audrey, a good friend, and Brian and Kathleen, Billy's mom and dad, were never made privy to Billy's incredible visions. Therefore, one day in early May, Audrey, playfully and somewhat wistfully brought up the subject of perhaps marrying Billy in the future. Billy's immediate reaction was one that he would almost immediately regret.

"Listen, Audrey, you know that I think the world of you. You're pretty, you're smart, you make me laugh all the time, and you're incredibly nice."

Audrey peered at Billy quizzically before responding.

"Well, those are all good things, but?"

There was a significant pregnant pause.

Billy took a deep breath before replying.

"But I can never marry you, Audrey."

Audrey appeared almost bemused, as if Billy was prefacing a punch line for some sort of joke.

"And why not?"

Audrey's face was a combination of intrigue, confusion and expectation.

"Because I already know who I'm going to marry well, sort of."

Audrey appeared hurt and fairly bewildered and replied softly. "What?"

Billy answered, but with a considerable amount of trepidation. He was about to tell the first person other than Pete Hamill of a frequent dream he experienced.

"I know who I'm going to marry, Audrey. I've dreamed about her many times."

Tears welled in Audrey's eyes.

"Who is she? Do I know her?"

By this time, Billy realized that he should have never initiated the conversation, but had no alternative but to continue it.

"I've never met her, Audrey. I don't even know her name."

Audrey sobbed briefly, but composed herself to respond.

"Is this some sort of sick joke? It's not funny, Billy."

"I'm sorry, Audrey. I'm just telling you the truth. I'm sorry if I hurt you."

Audrey responded with a combination of anger, confusion and hurt. "Hurt me?! Hurt me?! You're going to marry some imaginary girl?! Are you sick, Billy?"

Billy Farrell hung his head. For the initial time since he began having these visions, he realized how ridiculously absurd they appeared to a sentient being.

Audrey ran out of the room crying. She would not attend the senior prom with Billy. Billy, in fact, would not attend the prom. When Audrey's mother asked why Billy was not taking her daughter to the prom, Audrey responded, "He's with his imaginary girlfriend."

Chapter Ten

In the early morning hours of Friday, November 22, 1963, Billy awoke from his slumber. He had gone to bed the night before suffering from a severe head cold. He had overslept. It was approximately 8:00 A.M. and as he arose from bed, Billy's shirt was soaked with sweat. Billy was practically hyperventilating as he cried out, "Oh, my God!"

Billy had experienced a horrific dream, but all that he could recall was seeing a motorcade traveling through downtown Dallas, Texas. His dear friend Pete Hamill was now in Europe, most likely in Paris or London, and the local time there was early afternoon. Billy was in complete panic mode. This was a time way before the advent of cell phones.

Billy had, of course, never notified anyone other than Hamill of his dreams, visions that had all come true. How in hell could he possibly reach anyone in order to prevent this atrocious act from taking place? Would they come and place him in a strait jacket? Would they think him complicit because of his prior knowledge?

Billy searched for the telephone number Pete had given him before he relocated to Europe. Upon finding it, Billy dialed it feverishly, but got Hamill's answering machine. The overwrought Billy left a brief fearful message.

"Pete, it's Billy. Please dear God, get back to me as soon as humanly possible. Something truly awful is going to occur today in Dallas today and I don't know what time it will happen. I don't know who else to call, Pete. I don't know who else to trust. I attempted to reach you at the offices of *The Saturday Evening Post*, but all I got was an answering machine."

It was approximately 11:30 A.M. EST when Billy's telephone rang. He answered it breathlessly.

"Pete?!"

"Yes, Billy, it's me. Are you sure?"

"Hell, I haven't had one that didn't come true yet, Pete. What the hell do I do?!"

"Just hang tight. I'll attempt to reach Secret Service. I've already tried the White House to no avail. Shit, even I'm not sure what to tell them if I reach them, Billy. If I get through, I'll do everything in my power to keep you anonymous. Damn, how do we do this? I don't want to endanger you or anyone else, Billy."

"Pete, we're talking about the President of the United States. If you have to divulge your source, it's all right. I can live with it."

All communications to the White House and the Secret Service were shut down on that fateful day. Pete Hamill never got through, so additional conspiracy theories abound. Later on, Pete Hamill consoled Billy over the telephone, as Billy wept openly.

The JFK assassination, which affected all people who lived through it, in so many ways, forever altered lives. It was truly the end of the age of innocence.

Billy asked his older, but still young friend.

"Pete, can one change the future?"

"Billy, I'm not certain we can change the present."

Chapter Eleven

After over two years abroad, Pete Hamill left his job with *The Saturday Evening Post* and returned to the United States in order to resume his journalistic career with the *New York Post*. Pete had dearly missed his home in New York City and longed for the daily excitement in the greatest city in the world, despite all of its warts.

One of the first people Hamill contacted upon his returning was his younger friend Billy Farrell. It was late 1965 and the world had changed, and not for the better. Billy, now twenty years of age, was now in his senior year of college at NYU and had already passed the computer based test and physical ability test in order to become a NYC Firefighter. However, he would have to wait until he fulfilled the requirement of being twenty-one years old in order to join. Meanwhile, he furthered his education.

Billy continued to have dreams about the beautiful dark-haired girl with the round face. He began to have serious doubts as to whether or not he'd ever meet her and on occasion, if she actually existed.

Meanwhile, his friend, Pete Hamill, was building a reputation as a great columnist with the *New York Post*. There were thousands of New York City inhabitants who would await Hamill's daily columns with the same eager anticipation of watching their favorite ballplayers and theatrical stars. Hamill's columns were topical, controversial, and hard hitting in their impact and often brutal honesty. Hamill did not pull any of his punches.

Billy's visions of the dark-haired girl persisted, as her visage would now appear to him nightly. She was astoundingly beautiful, he thought. He wondered if he would ever actually meet her.

When Billy turned twenty-one years of age in February of 1966, he joined the ranks of the FDNY. He had achieved his goal of being a firefighter. Now that Billy was a man, Pete Hamill invited him to go drinking with him to various NYC watering holes and in the process, Billy, still addicted to great journalism, met some of the most extraordinary writers of the era. Hamill introduced him to George Kimball, who had been nominated for a Pulitzer Prize in Journalism and was one of the more intriguing characters of his time, and to legends such as Jimmy Breslin, Dick Young, Charles Pierce, joel oppenheimer of the ***Village Voice*** and many other literary greats. All enjoyed his company, as Billy was both erudite and knowledgeable in regard to their work.

Drinking was both the enjoyment and bane of many of these gentlemen's existence. Pete Hamill's candid introspection, ***A Drinking Life***, covered that subject as well as any book ever written.

Billy spent many hours with these legends at gin mills such as **"The Lion's Head,"** a renowned Greenwich Village hangout of some of the giants of literature. As Pete Hamill wrote in *A Drinking Life*, "I don't think many New York bars ever had such a glorious mixture of newspapermen, painters, musicians, seamen, ex-communists, priests and nuns, athletes, stockbrokers, politicians and folksingers, bound together in the leveling democracy of drink."

It was at the Lion's Head that Billy and Hamill had a deep conversation about Billy's gift, if that is what it was.

"So, Pete, you told me earlier that you believe that we cannot change the future and you mentioned that you weren't even certain we could even change the present?"

"William, you mentioned that your dreams and visions were becoming more frequent. Perhaps you're the one who **CAN** change the future. Maybe some great entity has given you this gift for a reason. Have you ever given consideration to the possibility that you were chosen? After all, no one else is experiencing these images."

"I wish I knew, Pete. I'm just an average guy, a firefighter just trying to get by. Truthfully, these visions I get, they often frighten me. I mean, why me?"

"That's a conundrum, my friend. Maybe you're being prepared for something truly great, Billy."

"Pete, seriously, what could possibly be greater than the Amoros catch in '55 that saved the World Series for the Brooklyn Dodgers?!"

Pete Hamill laughed as he lifted his glass in a proposed toast. "To Sandy Amoros and the Brooklyn Dodgers!"

Pete Hamill stared down at the empty glass in his hand. His face became a serious mask.

"I can't even alter the present. I've seen what this stuff does to people, Billy. I realize I'm an alcoholic. I've seen what drink has done to my own family."

The bartender filled Pete's glass and knocked on the wooden bar with his clenched fist.

"This one's on the house, Pete."

Pete once more stared at the glass in his hand before continuing. "Billy, I'm almost afraid to ask, but have your visions included anything about my future?"

Billy smiled before responding.

"Actually, Pete, my visions seem to cease in the early twenty-first century. And for the record, you're still alive, writing and thriving."

Pete Hamill raised his glass, smiled, and replied, "Well, that at least means I made it to sixty-five! Therefore, I guess it's safe to down this drink! Here's to the accuracy of your dreams, Billy! And great luck with your career in firefighting. We need more men like you!"

The two great friends downed their beverages.

CHAPTER TWELVE

It was Pete Hamill who saw her first. In 1967, Pete had made a trip to Paris to write a piece about a jazz musician for ***Esquire* Magazine**. On the evening before his flight home to the U.S., Hamill was invited to an exhibition of gymnastics at the Palais Des Sports. Hamill's seats were approximately seventy-five feet from the athletes and he had a clear view of the competitors. Various sports were represented, but it was the women's tumbling competition that captured his attention.

The crowd grew suddenly excited upon hearing the introduction of one of the participants, a Jennifer Swanson from Illinois in the United States. While full-bodied tumblers competed, without warning, a wheelchair emerged from one of the tunnels leading to the arena. Pete saw the young woman exit the wheelchair; he could only view her peripherally until she turned and faced him. Pete thought to himself, "I've seen her face, but where?"

Then he noticed for the initial time that the young lady was legless. At once, he recalled exactly where he had seen her face. His friend, the NYPD's sketch artist Ed Barrow, had drawn her face based on the description given to him by Billy Farrell! He had found the girl of his friend's dreams! She truly exists, just as did all of the others in Billy's dreams.

Here she was competing successfully against full-bodied young women. Then Pete saw what was evident in the artist's sketch, which was implausibly accurate. Jennifer Swanson was stunningly beautiful. Jennifer won the event with an incredible exhibition of power tumbling, but all Pete could think of was his excitement over the prospect of telling Billy that he had found the girl of his dreams. She was real and she was beyond inspirational and lovely.

Pete made it a point to visit the young woman after the event was over. He decided to not inform her of his friend's dreams about her. Pete reasoned that it would somehow work out in some sort of natural process and not by informing her of a seemingly preposterous vision. Pete Hamill knew exactly what to ask her. "Jennifer, do you have plans of performing in the United States?" Jennifer flashed a brilliant smile and replied.

"Yes, in fact I'll be in New York City next week, at Madison Square Garden."

Chapter Thirteen

Upon arriving back at Kennedy Airport, Pete dialed Billy's telephone number excitedly. Billy answered and spoke first.

"You saw her! You met her!"

"How in hell did you know?!"

Billy laughed before responding.

"How do you think?"

"Oh, my God, you had another dream!"

"It was vivid, Pete. I even saw you there."

Billy paused before continuing.

"In the dream, Pete, you introduced us at Madison Square Garden. Therefore, I fully expect you to attend the event with me on Friday evening."

"Billy, I'd be honored. Damn, am I in the Twilight Zone, or what?"

"I think we all are, Pete. Hey, I hope she likes me."

"Wait, Billy, how can she not like you? She's going to marry you, right?"

Billy laughed.

"At least that's what was in my dream, but Pete, other than the church altar vision and seeing her visage on countless occasions, I've never spoken to her or heard her speak to me. I'm nervous as all hell."

"Just let nature take its course."

Pete hesitated before asking. "Billy, you've seen her body, right? I mean, in the dream last evening, you saw more than just her face, right?"

"You mean the legless part? Pete, we've met so many brainless people, why not marry a beautiful legless girl?"

"I can't believe you're talking about marrying a girl you haven't met!"

"Pete, do you ever think your life would have been less weird if I never showed up at your office in 1961?"

"We live in New York City, my friend, we live and breathe weirdness. It is an integral part of our existence."

Chapter Fourteen

Billy's heart was palpitating as he entered the main entrance of Madison Square Garden on Eighth Avenue and 50th Street. It would be the last year of the old Garden, as the new Garden would open in 1968. Pete Hamill decided to cover the event for the *New York Post*. It was just another excuse concocted in order to introduce Billy to Jennifer Swanson.

Many of those in attendance were not well versed or educated in the nuances of gymnastics, however, when they saw Jennifer introduced as a participant, they all cheered wildly. New Yorkers are renowned for being champions of the underdogs. Therefore, seeing Jennifer in her wheelchair elicited an extremely warm and favorable response. Little did the majority of the crowd realize that Jennifer was considered one of the more accomplished of the competitors.

One can only begin to imagine what was going through Billy's mind as he anticipated the alleged inevitable. Here he was, about to meet a young woman who had dominated his dreams since the age of six. Now, at twenty-two years of age and a grown man, he began to doubt his sanity. After all, he had actually dreamed that this was to be his wife. How can any sentient being rationalize the absurdity of such a possibility? What if she wasn't even remotely attracted to him? However, everything else he had visions of came to be reality.

And then another logical thought came to him. What would he say to her? Does she actually already KNOW him? I mean, why else, did she invariably appear in his dreams. Did she plan this? Is this some sort of diabolical scheme and if so, who is the author of such a plot?

Billy's emotions ran the full gamut. There was excitement, fear, dread, anticipation, wonderment, confusion, and a sense of the absurd. Was there a grander scheme involved? Was this some sort of a master plan drawn up by some higher entity? Billy was raised a devout Catholic, however, this seemed like nothing he'd ever heard in his upbringing.

One brief thought invading Billy's thoughts was that of the possibility of Jennifer being malevolent. Did she have any connection whatsoever to the outcome of his dreams? After all, there was the horrific vision of JFK's assassination. However, Billy then thought of Sandy Amoros's incredible catch vision. Certainly, there was no malice in that.

The arrival of Pete Hamill on the floor of Madison Square Garden more than slightly assuaged Billy's apprehension and fear. Pete glanced up at Billy in his seat at "courtside" and smiled. Billy nodded and shrugged his shoulders which elicited a laugh from Hamill. Pete attempted to imagine what Billy was feeling, but of course, knowingly fell considerably short.

Prior to her performance, Jennifer's arrival in her wheelchair was met with significant applause from the crowd. As Jennifer climbed out of her seat and onto the mat she would be competing on, Billy saw at once her beautiful round face and any thoughts of her perhaps being malevolent vanished from his mind. Billy thought Jennifer was the most beautiful girl he had ever seen and thought it surreal that the girl who had invaded his dreams actually existed.

Near the conclusion of the show, Pete signaled for Billy to join him on the floor of Madison Square Garden. Hamill spoke briefly with a security guard who allowed Billy to enter. Pete led Billy to a tunnel which led to the area where the competitors had gathered to meet the media.

"Are you all right, Buddy?"

Billy laughed before responding.

"I guess I'm as good as I'm going to be considering I'm a participant in some sort of mystical dream. This is akin to an out of body experience, I would imagine. It's as if I'm watching myself."

Jennifer Swanson was concluding an interview with a WINS reporter as Pete and Billy approached. At once, she recognized Pete, who she had met the prior week in Paris. Jennifer smiled and extended her hand to Pete and spoke.

"It's Pete, right? It's nice to see you again."

Jennifer had yet to notice Billy who stood a mere five feet away and slightly behind the beauty's wheelchair.

Jennifer continued, "Did you enjoy the show? I goofed on one of my tumbles."

Jennifer giggled as Pete responded.

"I loved the show, Jennifer, but I can fit what I know about your sport on the head of a pin. I apologize if that offends you."

Jennifer giggled once more, a chuckle which tugged at Billy's heartstrings. He loved her voice.

"I'm not offended at all. I'm just pleased you enjoyed watching. Oh, and call me Jen. My friends call me Jen."

Pete Hamill placed his hand on Jennifer's shoulder before replying. "All right then, Jen it is. Jen, I'd like to introduce you to a dear friend of mine, Billy Farrell."

Jennifer turned slightly to her left and upon seeing Billy for the initial time, her facial expression changed completely. Although her smile dissipated, she appeared slightly perplexed, as if she were attempting to determine what or who she was looking at.

"Do I know you? Have we met?"

Billy had no idea how to respond. He briefly searched in his mind for the proper response. Finally, he settled for what he hoped would suffice. He was not about to inform her that she occupied his dreams for nearly two decades.

"I doubt it. I would have remembered someone as astoundingly lovely as you."

Jennifer blushed and giggled before responding.

"You really do look familiar. Perhaps I saw you in a dream." Jennifer's reaction caught Billy entirely off guard. It was the last thing he'd expected. It jolted him to his core.

Jennifer noticed the fact that Billy seemed suddenly impacted, but did not associate the affect with what she had said.

"Are you all right, Billy? You seem a bit shaken."

Billy attempted to regain his composure; however, although in perfectly excellent health, he suddenly collapsed onto the floor.

Chapter Fifteen

As Billy lay in his bed at Lenox Hill Hospital in Manhattan, he began to flutter his eyelids. As he became cognizant of his surroundings, he immediately saw Pete Hamill seated next to his bed.

"You're going to be okay, Ace, but you gave us all a scare. All your tests came back negative, especially the one on your brain."

Billy laughed and asked how long he'd been there.

"Just a few hours and you'll be released first thing in the morning. They're just holding you for observation."

Pete peered briefly over his shoulder before continuing. Well, I'm going to call it a night. I've got to show up at the *New York Post* offices in the morning, but you're not going to be alone for long. You have a visitor."

Billy straightened up in his bed and peered towards the door as Jennifer Swanson wheeled herself into the room. Jen smiled sweetly before remarking.

"You're not going to faint on me again, are you? You're about to give me some sort of complex. Do I have that affect on you?"

Jen's giggle made Billy tingle.

"No, I promise not to keel over again. Gosh, I'm so sorry I ruined your evening. The only effect you have on me is the fact you're extraordinarily beautiful."

Jen giggled before replying.

"Well, in that case, you should ask me out on a date."

Billy's next thought was the dream in which he lifted her veil at the church altar and saw her beautiful face in his wondrous dream.

"Will you go out with me, Jen?"

"Yeah, yes I will. I'd like that very much."

Billy and Jennifer stared into each other's eyes for several moments before Jen broke the silence.

"Are you certain we've never met before, Billy?"

"Actually, Jen, I'm not that clear. Perhaps in that dream you mentioned."

Jen reached for Billy's hand and held it tightly.

"Billy, what do you do? Our conversation at Madison Square Garden was interrupted by some guy fainting."

"I'm just a firefighter, Jen."

Jen giggled before jokingly scolding.

"Just? Just?! Just a firefighter? You're a hero, Billy. You save lives and protect us."

Less than a year later, Billy and Jen were married and another of

Billy's dreams bore fruition. Billy reenacted the scene in his dream when he lifted Jen's veil and embellished it by kissing her beautiful round face.

The young couple settled in Billy and Pete's beloved New York City.

Chapter Sixteen

Following his marriage to beautiful Jen, although Billy ceased dreaming about her, his other visions increased in volume and intensity. There were frequent dreams of happenings in and around New York City, and with his friend, Pete, making occasional sojourns to Vietnam where he covered the unpopular war, Billy was sure to remind his friend that he had visions of Pete alive and well and writing in the early twenty-first century. Not that Hamill would have been influenced by danger as he had become one of the leading journalistic voices against what he considered an unjust war. Pete had literally been added to "An Enemies List" of Richard Nixon's White House, part of a group of journalists, performers, celebrities, and other media people who were opposed to the war. However, Billy made sure to report all of his visions to Pete because of the fact that he seemed more concerned about his friend's well being than he was. As Pete reported from his many journeys to Vietnam, "I discovered I wasn't afraid of death."

In April of 1969, Billy experienced another vivid dream about baseball. This time it revolved around the New York Mets, the perpetual doormat of the National League and the laughing stock of baseball. The Mets, nearly always finishing in last place, were expected to be slightly improved in 1969, but certainly not a playoff contender and most definitely not a World Series winner, but that is what Billy dreamed. Not only did Billy's vision include a trip to the fall classic, but a World Series victory versus the formidable American powerhouse, the Baltimore Orioles.

When Pete was alerted of what was to occur with the Mets later that season, he reasoned that Billy's clairvoyance had sprung a leak. "It's time to get a lube job for your brain, William."

However, led by former 1955 Brooklyn Dodgers superstar Gil Hodges as their manager, the Mets behind an array of outstanding young pitchers and an unlikely blend of veteran players and untested youngsters, managed to win both the pennant and the World Series. Both Pete and Billy wondered aloud when exactly these dreams would finally conclude. And despite the fact that Billy was deeply in love with Jen, he decided never to tell her of his visions or the fact that she dominated them for so many years.

In the late '60s, Billy and Jennifer welcomed their two children into the world, Peter, named after Hamill, and Angela, named after African American civil rights activist, Angela Davis. The kids grew to be intelligent, thoughtful and attractive children. Life was perfect, and despite having a few close calls while firefighting, Billy, having been given commendations for bravery on three occasions, managed to escape with minor abrasions and injuries.

Chapter Seventeen

By 1977, Billy and Jen had the perfect marriage and resided in an East Greenwich Village flat with their children, Peter, eight, and Angela, six. Billy had recently been promoted from Lieutenant to the rank of Captain, and his popularity with his co-workers made him a strong candidate for the eventual position of Battalion Chief.

One Friday during the school year of 1977, Angela, the younger of the siblings, arrived home from school in tears. Peter, her slightly older brother's entrance was also troubling. Peter entered the house sporting a black eye; his shirt was ripped and his knuckles were scraped. Upon seeing her kids in disarray, Jen immediately followed them to their rooms and asked what had occurred and if they were all right.

Peter responded that he was fine and that he didn't want to talk about it and little Angela just nodded her head as Jen attempted successfully to stifle her tears by holding her. After Angela had calmed down, Jen took both children into the bathroom in order to tend to them. After drying Angela's tears and applying a damp washcloth to the insignificant injuries suffered by Peter, she fed the children their dinner and sent them to their rooms to watch television. Jen would send Billy in to investigate once he arrived home from the fire station. Angela, in particular, was extremely close with her father, and Jen reasoned correctly that he'd manage to find out what had happened. Pete Hamill, still a great friend of the family, was to be a dinner guest that evening.

When Billy arrived home early that evening, Jen advised him of the situation. Billy's initial stop was to see his daughter, Angela, since he was aware that his son, Peter, was often too proud to confide any possible weaknesses, emotionally or physically. In Little League baseball, Billy once watched as Peter took a hard pitch to his wrist from a hard-throwing wild left-handed pitcher and he noted that his brave son absolutely refused medical attention and fought back tears.

Upon entering Angela's room, Billy asked, "Are you all right, Princess?"

Angela replied by shaking her head affirmatively, but not speaking. "I'll be right back, angel. Everything will be all right."

Angela smiled and Billy left the room.

Billy entered Peter's room and gently said, "That's quite a shiner you've got there, son. I'm sort of hoping that the other guy looks worse."

"I got in a few shots, Dad."

Billy smiled and responded. "I hope you had a good reason, son."

"I did, Dad, honest."

"I believe you, Peter."

Billy then re-entered Angela's room and sat down next to her on her bed. On Angela's wall was a large photograph of her mom tumbling in an exhibition and another of her mom high up in the air in an acrobatic pose.

"Do you want to talk about it, sweetheart?"

Angela, a little round-faced pretty brunette, reminiscent of the visage of her mom who appeared in Billy's dreams years ago, slowly shook her head negatively.

Billy kissed his daughter's forehead and spoke softly.

"If you tell me why you were so upset, angel, I'm not promising I can fix it, but I cannot even try if I don't know what it is. I promise to do anything I can to make you feel better. It really bothers me whenever you cry, honey. No matter what it was that upset you, Mommy and Daddy love you very much."

With that, little Angela began sobbing once more. Suddenly, Angela blurted out, "Mikey said that Mommy was a freak! He called her half a mommy!"

Billy held Angela in his arms.

"Angela, sweetheart, your mommy is the greatest and most beautiful mommy in the entire world. She's a champion, too. She can do more things than anyone else's mommy. And I love both of you with all my heart. It doesn't matter what mean people say, Angela. They're just words and words cannot hurt us. Now, give me a big hug and a smile, Princess."

Angela leaped out of her bed and into her father's arms. Billy pointed to the photos of Jen on the walls.

"Look at your mommy. She's a great athlete and she's the most beautiful mommy in the whole universe. I'd like to see Mikey's mother even attempt to do what Mommy can do!"

Billy hesitated before continuing.

"Don't let anyone's words ever hurt you, Princess. Okay?"

"Okay, Daddy, I'll try."

"Good. Do you know what happened to your brother?"

"Yeah, Daddy, but please don't be angry with him. He beat Mikey up."

Billy smiled before responding.

"I promise not to be angry with Peter, angel. I don't like for either of you to fight, but it sure sounds as if Mikey had it coming to him. Sleep well, Princess. And if any of the kids ever says anything mean to you, just tell me, okay?"

Angela smiled and answered, "Okay, Daddy, I love you!"

"I love you, Princess!"

CHAPTER EIGHTEEN

Pete Hamill arrived for dinner at 7:00 P.M. He had just completed his latest novel, *Flesh and Blood*, about the brutality of boxing. The *New York Times* review stated, "A taut, punchy read. Hamill writes stark, staccato sentences designed to sting, building suspense that is rooted in character... Makes "Rocky" seem like a fairy tale." Pete Hamill was clearly at the top of his game.

At dinner that evening, Billy, Jen and Hamill discussed poor Angela's ordeal at school earlier that day. Hamill also smiled as he was made aware of how her older brother, Peter, came to his sister's defense against a larger child.

"He apparently acquitted himself quite well, especially when considering the abrasions on his knuckles. You not only named him after me, but it appears as if your son has inherited some of my earlier traits."

Billy laughed uproariously before responding.

"Earlier traits? I seem to recall seeing someone who looked exactly like you get into a brawl at ringside just a short while ago!"[2]

Pete winced before replying.

"Touché! Guilty as charged."

Pete Hamill then changed his expression to one of seriousness. "You know, humiliation, and that's what it was for both little Angela and Billy, can persuade

[2] Hamill indeed, was involved in a melee at ringside, one in which he pounded out six thugs with thunderous left hooks after the men had made untoward remarks about a lovely Puerto Rican woman seated at ringside. The woman, Ramona Negron, was at the time the girlfriend of the great boxer, Jose "Chegui" Torres, a dear and close personal friend of Hamill's. Hamill would eventually marry Ramona. They have since divorced.

you to commit semi-violent acts. Your kids are too young to fully understand how unimaginably great their mom is."

Jen sat straight up and replied, "Aw, I'm blushing. Thanks, Pete."

Pete continued, "Hell, I've even retaliated with hurtful and venomous words in my columns and more often than I'd like to admit. It's a method I developed in the streets of Brooklyn growing up."

Billy replied after shaking his head, "Pete, the great majority of the people you verbally assault had it coming. There is nothing wrong with being sensitive to injustice."

"Thanks, William, but on occasion I've actually regretted some of the things I've written. Keep in mind that the printed word really cannot be retracted. You can apologize in print, but folks will only remember the original words. Printed words are permanent."

Jen immediately replied, "Yes, but in your case, Pete, you're building an enormously great legacy of being fair and open-minded. No one can be 100 percent perfect. Not even you."

Pete Hamill took a sip of the drink in his hand before responding. "Thanks, Jen, but you guys are a bit biased.[3] The humiliation that both Angela and Peter suffered today will only make them stronger. You know, I grew up in a state of rage. My mom, Anne, and my dad, Bill, were poor. I loved my mother dearly and I grew to respect my dad, eventually. I would explode into violence, my hands clenched into fists, hammering and battering at people I did not even know. The violence was always white and blind and savage, and when I think about the cause of it now, it always seemed to involve humiliation. I remember one cold winter afternoon when I was fourteen. I had won a scholarship to a Jesuit high school called Regis, which was a long subway ride from Brooklyn. Most of the students were upper middle class, and I spent the first few months there in a state of desperate unhappiness. I imagined Regis as a place where older boys shared a democratic camaraderie with younger boys, where you learned from one another. Instead, I found a place stinking with class rank and privilege and a student body that was, in retrospect, docile and cliquish. One rainy winter day, I arrived at school soaked by the walk from Lexington Avenue. There were large holes in the bottom of my shoes. I did not own a pair of galoshes; instead, cardboard had been stuffed into the shoes. When I went into the locker room,

[3] (from "Irrational Ravings" by Pete Hamill, G.P. Putnam's Sons, 1971)

my shoes were squishing with rainwater. I found a piece of cardboard in a wastebasket and sat down on a bench and took my shoes off. I was tearing the cardboard to fit the shoes when I heard laughter. I looked up to see a couple of juniors snickering and giggling at my shoes. I felt humiliated and grubby and helpless. I sat in class like a bomb, and when school was over, I waited down the street in the rain in a doorway on Park Avenue, until I saw one of the young men who had laughed. I exploded in a fury of punching, kicking, and stomping and left the kid smashed and bleeding on the sidewalk, before I ran off in the rain. I didn't go to school for two days, because I was frightened and somehow ashamed. Ever since, it has been impossible for me to watch a black kid walk into a white school without wondering if he had cardboard in his shoes. Ever since, I've been afraid of the murderer who lives in my body."

Both Billy and Jen sat enthralled as Pete Hamill continued.

"But there was more to the anger than poverty. There was something in me that wanted the world to be fair. I grew up hearing stories of the injustices in Northern Ireland, where my folks were from. There were stories of what the Protestant landlords were doing to Catholic AND Protestant workers. That led to a kind of rude sympathy for underdogs, for blacks, Puerto Ricans and Indians, for the damaged and the lost, which was further deepened by the fact that as a young man in America my father had lost a leg playing soccer. In the years when I was growing up, my father had a street fighter's sense of bigotry; he wouldn't let anyone use the words 'nigger' or 'spic' in the house, and once, when I was about eleven, I used the word 'kike' at the dinner table, and he leaned over and smacked my face brutally and said, 'Benny Leonard was a kike.' I didn't know that Benny Leonard was a Jew off the Lower East Side who had become the greatest of all lightweight champions of the world, but I never used the word 'kike' again. It is a simple matter to sneer at that story, at its lack of sophistication or its possibly patronizing implications. But it was the way you learned things in that neighborhood, and I thank the old man for doing what he did. He would never have described himself as 'liberal.' He simply hated unfairness, bigotry, and the absence of justice."

Jen smiled as she refilled Pete Hamill's glass before responding. "Wow, perhaps I can convince you to have a long talk with the kids."

Pete Hamill laughed and retorted.

"Thanks, however, I strongly suspect, actually I *know*, that you will handle it perfectly, just as you manage everything else in your lives."

Pete then concluded with.

"Just know this; I truly feel empathy for both little Peter and Angela. But having parents like you and Billy, I know they're in the greatest of hands."

Chapter Nineteen

On the morning of November 24, 1971, Pete Hamill answered his phone to hear Billy laughing hysterically. Between guffaws, Billy managed to compose himself in order to be slightly less unintelligible.

"Pete, this one you're not going to believe!"

"What, did Spiro Agnew utter something intelligent?"

"Pete, this one's a beauty! This is the weirdest dream I've ever had. I have never laughed so hard in my life. I hope you're sitting down, because this one is so implausible, it's entirely absurd. Mel Brooks couldn't have created this spectacle. A plane is going to be hijacked today."

Pete hesitated before responding.

"And this is supposed to be funny?"

"Wait, you've got to hear this, Pete. It was as vivid a dream as I've ever had. It was as if I was aboard the plane! Don't worry, no one gets hurt. Not only that, the dream included the future. This guy, the hijacker becomes a hero! A folk hero. There will be books and songs written about him."

"So, I shouldn't alert the authorities?"

"Pete, honest, I wouldn't. Besides, not only doesn't anyone get hurt, but even the people onboard won't know they're in any imminent danger. Hell, again, if we alerted the authorities, I'd be found out and who is going to believe that I can see the future. I'd be arrested for complicity in the skyjacking. I mean, how in hell would I know about it in advance? Besides, I don't want this guy to get caught, and he won't! Not now, not ever!"

Pete sighed, laughed and replied.

"I'm all ears. This may be the weirdest yet."

"Pete, you don't know the half of it. Get this, some schmegeggie named Dan Cooper is going to purchase an airline ticket in order to fly from Portland to Seattle. It's Flight #305 on a Boeing 727. It's got thirty-six people on board."

Pete laughed.

"You're beginning to frighten me, Billy."

"Get this, this Dan Cooper guy, and that's not his real name, no one will ever find out his real name, purchases this one way ticket at Northeast Orient's counter at the airport in Portland. He gets on the plane and is seated in the back of the passenger cabin in seat #18C. He lights a cigarette and orders a bourbon and soda."

Pete Hamill is now laughing so hard that he is practically convulsing. "Wait, you dreamed all of these minute details and you don't even know his real name?! You even know his seat number, but your vision didn't include the guy's actual name? Billy, I think your dream apparatus has finally imploded."

"Hear me out, this is hilarious. This Cooper guy, or whoever he is, passes a note to a flight attendant named Florence Schaffner, a real attractive doll."

"Billy, this is insane. You know the name of the flight attendant, but not the hijacker?!"

Billy laughs before continuing.

"Well, 'Cooper' passes her this note at just after 2:50 P.M., moments after the flight takes off. This Florence gal, remember she's hot, thinks he's flirting with her, so she shoves it in her purse without looking at it."

"You've really lost it this time, Billy."

"Well, 'Cooper' whispers to her, 'Miss, you'd better look at that note. I have a bomb.' It's supposedly in his briefcase. The note is all in upper case neatly printed letters. He motions to her to sit down next to him, the flight is not full, and he dictates his demands to her. He wants $200,000 in unmarked negotiable U.S. currency. (***that would be equivalent to well over a million dollars today) So, this Florence gal takes the note up to the cockpit and when she returns to Cooper, he is wearing dark sunglasses."

"Jesus, Billy, did you dream this in wide screen?!

Hamill is laughing.

"So, the pilot, some guy named William Scott, notifies Seattle-Tacoma Airport air traffic control, which in turn informs local and federal authorities."

Hamill laughs again.

"You even dreamed the pilot's name!"

"As I said, this was the most vivid dream to date, Pete. Now, this D.B. Cooper guy"

Pete interrupts.

"I thought you didn't know his name. D.B. Cooper?"

"Oh, that's another thing. Due to some News media communication error, his name was transcribed as 'D.B. Cooper.'"

Pete is now beside himself with laughter.

"Oh, sure, blame the media! It's my fault!"

"So, Cooper tells Florence to instruct the pilot to inform the passengers that everything is all right. The pilot makes an announcement that their arrival in Seattle would be delayed because of some "minor mechanical difficulty. Cooper is polite, calm, and well spoken. Cooper has demanded the $200,000 and a parachute. The aircraft circles Puget Sound for approximately two hours to allow Seattle police and the FBI to assemble Cooper's parachute and ransom money and to mobilize emergency personnel."

"You're serious, Billy, this Cooper is going to get away with it!"

"Yes, isn't it delicious? Cooper actually orders another bourbon and water and attempts to give this Florence gal the change!"

"Don't tell me, she cannot accept because of airline regulations!" "Yes, yes!! Isn't this great? Well, Cooper demands 10,000 unmarked $20 bills, but he rejects the military issue parachute offered by McChord Air Force Base. The plane has now landed in Seattle. Cooper insists on civilian parachutes with manually operated rip chords."

Pete laughs and replies.

"Brilliant!"

"Well, Seattle police get the parachutes from a local skydiving school. Once the delivery is completed, Cooper allows all passengers, Florence and the other flight attendant, Alice Hancock, to exit the plane. Donald Nyrop, Northeast Orient's president, authorizes the payment of the ransom and ordered all employees to fully cooperate with Cooper. At 7.40 P.M., the plane takes off with Cooper, the pilot William Scott, a flight attendant named Mucklow, co-pilot Rataczak, and flight engineer H.E. Anderson aboard."

"Jesus, Billy, you've got me rooting for this guy, Cooper!"

"Well, while they were refueling on the runway, Cooper tells the entire crew to enter the cockpit and close the door. At 8:13 P.M., the aircraft's tail section sustains a sudden upward movement."

Pete reacts excitedly.

"Don't tell me, the SOB parachuted!"

"Yes, yes!!!! The crazy bastard is wearing a business suit and he's got the cash in a knapsack! But my dream doesn't end. It extends to the very beginning of the twenty-first century. Like I said, Pete, all my dreams seem to stop there. Well, Cooper, or whatever his name is, gets away with it. There are songs written about him."

"Billy, if this comes true, I may write a song about him!"

Billy laughs before concluding.

"Well, of course, there's an extensive FBI manhunt. The plane was headed to Mexico City according to Cooper's commands, but he bailed out somewhere in the Pacific Northwest. The FBI conducts this lengthy investigation and I believe it was still ongoing entering the twenty-first century. And get this, they stated that the perpetrator, and they never actually learned his actual name, had never been located or identified. At one time the FBI surmised he didn't survive his jump, but neither the parachute nor the cash was ever found."

"Billy, I'll be glued to the news reports today."

Pete's demeanor changed briefly to being serious.

"William, did you ever consider undergoing some sort of neurological testing?"

"Actually, I have, Pete, but I honestly fear that if the CIA ever became aware of this curse, or gift, or whatever it is I have, they'd most likely lock me in a room somewhere and use me for nefarious reasons. They'd most likely claim I had disappeared."

"I agree, Billy, this will have to remain a secret for our entire lives, I suppose."

Later that day, Pete Hamill while watching the news reports, sat there in disbelief as the exact events that Billy foretold, became reality. Pete headed to "Rattigan's Bar" to get sufficiently inebriated. He drank numerous toasts to "D.B. Cooper."

Chapter Twenty

Following little Angela's humiliating experience in grade school, the one in which she came home sobbing because an older boy had made fun of her mom, neither Billy or Jen were aware of any additional incidents regarding her physical appearance.

Jen had been born with the condition, a birth defect that was unexplainable. However, having no legs never deterred Jen from living a full and remarkable life. She was otherworldly beautiful, had competed successfully versus full-bodied athletes, and, of course, was raising a family of her own with absolutely zero difficulty. Jennifer Farrell, nee Jennifer Swanson, was inspirational beyond belief. Peter, now eighteen years of age in the year 1987, was particularly proud of his mother's accomplishments and extremely protective of her image. Peter, with hope of being a law enforcement officer, was also highly protective of his lovely little sister, Angela, now sixteen and in high school. Peter would actually ask his mom various questions about her youth and how she coped with the seeming disadvantage of having no legs. Jen would always answer truthfully, that since she was born with the condition, it posed no hindrance whatsoever, and that if she had to live life over again, she'd remain legless. Jen was, of course, speaking the truth.

Angela, a bit more reserved than her older brother, would never discuss her mom's alleged physical disability with her or anyone else, for that matter. Angela never brought any of her friends over to the house and often Jen would wonder if it were because of the humiliation she suffered when the older boy had made cruel remarks about her condition. Not wanting to press the subject that Jen reasoned may result in emotional distress for her daughter, Jen never brought the matter up.

Angela's closest friend in high school was Sharon Carswell, an absolutely stunning sixteen-year-old African American girl. Sharon was not only beautiful, but she was the most popular girl in Angela's classes. Sharon, seemingly near perfect, was a great student and admired by all of her classmates and teachers. Her beauty combined with her ebullience made her the apple of everyone's eye. Sharon had no enemies on the planet.

One day, in the midst of her junior year, Sharon, however, was involved in a horrific car crash. Although injuries were suffered by both her parents and younger brother, Sharon's injuries were the most significant. Sharon lie in a hospital for several weeks and her life hung in the balance. Sharon eventually pulled through, however, her left leg, which had been pinned and crushed in the accident, had to be amputated. Sharon's young world had shattered, and although she had been fitted for a prosthetic, she was having an enormously difficult time in dealing with her misfortune; she was disconsolate. Sharon, an honor student, was also a tremendous athlete, a captain of both the volleyball team and a track and field star.

Angela was extremely concerned as her closest friend became withdrawn to the point of being almost a recluse. Sharon, normally a great student, would just go through the motions in class as if she were merely fulfilling an obligation, her demeanor being doleful. Sharon normally would participate and often be the leader of various school organizations, but now, after classes concluded, she would immediately go home with nary a word to anyone. Angela had lost her best friend and confidante. Both young ladies, super intelligent and thoughtful, were inseparable. Inseparable, that is, until the life-altering calamity.

Jen, of course, had heard about the catastrophe; it had been all over the news; however, with her daughter being independent and not given to sharing her innermost thoughts, really had no idea how well she knew her classmate.

"Angela, how well do you know the poor girl involved in the car crash the other day?"

Angela answered, a bit surprised that her mother would ask, since the teenager had never invited any of her classmates to their home. "Fairly well, Mom."

Of course, the answer was an understatement as Angela and Sharon were practically sisters and partook in a camaraderie that few share.

Angela not only grieved for Sharon's loss of self esteem, her sudden lack of confidence, and realized that she was not only losing her dearest friend, but also arrived at the conclusion that Sharon was losing herself, her wonderful persona and demeanor unrecognizable with little or no association with her past. Sharon had packed it in, quit on life, as it were.

One night, upon arriving home from school, Angela lay in bed and began to cry, lamenting the loss of her once great friend and empathizing with what she must feel. Then suddenly she thought of her mom, Jen.

A great revelation struck Angela as if it were a lightning bolt. Her mom, her wonderful mom! Never once had she seen her mom depressed, angry or even remotely upset about her condition. Never once did her mom discuss with her what it was like to have people staring at her in pity, sorrow, or wonder. No, her mom had the greatest disposition in the universe; she wore her "disability" as if it weren't, and therefore, it was not a disability or defect, it was a badge of honor. Angela's mom was perfect, she thought, and she was right. Angela immediately put in motion a plan to reclaim her best friend. She would not tell her mom about it; she would not have to, she reasoned.

CHAPTER TWENTY-ONE

Following school one afternoon, Angela approached Sharon and asked if she would come over for dinner that evening. Sharon, withdrawn and now suspicious, hesitated before responding. Sharon, of course, had never even seen Angela's mom, Jen, and was entirely unaware of the fact that her friend's mother had been born with a significant birth defect.

"No, thanks, Angie, I'm going home to read."

Angela sensed the insincerity in Sharon's voice and knew that her friend was merely avoiding her, as she avoided everyone else since her misfortune.

"Sharon, I really need your help. I'm having problems with calculus."

Angela had come up with a terrific white lie. In truth, Angela had struggled briefly with calculus, a subject much like all the others which Sharon had mastered from day one.

"I suppose, Angie. If you really need me."

Angela telephoned her mom and told her that a friend of hers would be joining them for dinner. Angela, of course, did not volunteer the name of her friend and Jen, respecting her daughter's privacy, did not inquire of the identity. However, upon seeing Sharon Carswell enter through the door, walking a bit unevenly on her prosthetic, Jen immediately ascertained who she was.

"Hi, Mom, this is my friend Sharon. She's going to help me with my calculus and have dinner with us."

Sharon at once noticed that Jen's mom, who was wheeling around the kitchen, had no legs. Sharon's mouth was agape although she wasn't aware of it. Sharon immediately noticed Jen's immense beauty and warmth.

"Welcome to our home, Sharon. Gosh, you're pretty!"

Sharon shyly thanked Angela's mom and replied, "Thanks, Mrs. Farrell. You're beautiful!"

Jen giggled before responding.

"Thanks, but I really think you're ridiculously attractive. I hope you like macaroni and cheese."

Sharon, smiling for the initial time in months, became animated and appeared to almost her ebullient self.

"I love macaroni and cheese!"

Before the evening was done, Sharon was enthralled at learning that her best friend's mom had been a gifted athlete who had successfully competed against full bodied women. Sharon viewed the photographs of Jen in amazement and wonder. Angela had regained her friend and Sharon began to emerge from her shell and return to being her outgoing and beloved self. Sharon became a regular guest at the Farrell's home and returned to class with a renewed outlook on life. Soon she would develop a self-deprecating personality and began telling jokes about her condition.

Sharon would go on to study law at Columbia University and went on to become a successful Corporate Law Attorney. To this day, she and Angela remain close friends.

Chapter Twenty-Two

"Sometimes the most terrible thing of all is to confirm what you have only imagined." – Pete Hamill

The decade of the 1980s was perhaps the most significant bridge between the world of the Baby Boomers' universe and what is widely considered "modern times." Although the decade saw great socioeconomic change due to advances in technology, it also ushered in that very same technology rendering our planet a much more perilous place.

The decade also heralded in the deadly AIDS epidemic, which would kill over 39 million people by the year 2013. Global warming became known to both the scientific and political community. However, perhaps even a greater concern was the survival of the human species on a more immediate level. The worldwide chasm between the haves and the have-nots actually widened to the extent that even in major metropolitan areas such as New York, homelessness reached a crisis point. Hopelessness and despair became an overwhelming factor in a multitude of lives, in both foreign and far too familiar places. One could not walk on a New York street and not see the expansive disparity between the advantaged and disadvantaged.

Terrorist attacks, although still not on the insane level of the second decade of the twenty-first century, were becoming far too frequent, and skirmishes and virtual wars in the Middle East were becoming the norm and not the exception. Extremist groups were gaining in power as serious wars broke out between fanatical religious factions, the Iran-Iraq war perhaps being the most foretelling.

It was in this world that Billy and Jen were raising their children, Peter and Angela, who became well-adjusted teenagers. By the end of the decade, Billy had now risen to the rank of Battalion Chief; however, he still looked forward to his retirement, as the days of fighting fires and rescuing people, although gratifying, were weighing on him emotionally. He had seen far too much and seen far too many lives lost and they included both the victims of infernos as well as several of his comrades.

When the year 1988 rolled around, Billy had fulfilled his twenty-two years of service for the FDNY. He had been awarded many citations and awards for bravery and had literally saved countless dozens of lives. After twenty-two years of service, a FDNY firefighter can retire regardless of his age and with full benefits. So, Billy became a civilian, which pleased both his still beautiful wife, Jen, and his son, Peter, now nineteen, and a sophomore at Columbia University, majoring in Criminology and Angela, now seventeen, and improbably as beautiful as her mom. Angela was in her junior year of high school.

Although Billy was retired from active duty, he remained close with his former compatriots and attended many of their functions and also retained a close relationship with their families. Billy, who had once considered journalism as a career, began to take English writing classes at NYU.

Meanwhile, his dear friend, Pete Hamill's career continued to flourish. Hamill, now fifty-three years of age and still ruggedly handsome and athletic, had written nine books, innumerable newspaper columns, had butted heads with countless blowhard politicians and officials, and was widely considered the greatest American columnist and one of the greatest novelists and autobiographical writers of his time.

Meantime, Billy's dreams persisted, but not as frequently as they had in earlier days. Billy was forty-three years of age and began to reassess exactly why he had been given such gifts. With more time on his hands than ever before, his prior dreams began to haunt him. He and Jen were as in love as the day they met, but she would often see Billy staring off into space, as if he were attempting to solve an age old mystery. Incredibly, he had never discussed any of his dreams with her or anyone other than Hamill, not even the dreams of her visage which had occupied his mind for his entire younger life.

Chapter Twenty-Three

The decade of the 1990s proved to be tumultuous. The Gulf War in Iraq dominated the news. In August of 1990, Iraqi forces invaded and conquered Kuwait. Oil was the most contentious consideration, as human life continued to be a non-negligible commodity. The UN condemned the action, and a coalition force led by the United States was sent to the Persian Gulf. These forces drove Iraq away from Kuwait in a mere four days. In the aftermath, the Kurds in the north and the Shiites to the south rose up in revolt. The United States eventually invaded in 2003, and Iraq was cut off from most of the world.

The first Chechen War took place between 1994-1996 between the Russian Federation and the Chechen Republic of Ichkeria. The second Chechen conflict began in 1999, and it is still ongoing.

There were genocides in Rwanda, unrest in Algeria and in the United States, race riots rocked Los Angeles. These riots resulted in 53 deaths and over 5500 property fires, and they were the result of an all-white jury acquitting four police officers of the brutal beating of a motorist named Rodney King. However, in 1993 all four police officers, three white and one Hispanic, were convicted in a federal civil rights case.

The war in Somalia commenced in 1991, and it is ongoing to this day, and in 1999, the Pakistan army overthrew the democratically elected government.

Terrorist attacks increased at an alarming rate, even here in the "safe" United States. There was the 1993 World Trade Center bombing and the bombing of a federal building in Oklahoma City in 1995, killing 168.

U.S. Naval military forces launched cruise missile attacks against Al-Qaeda bases in Afghanistan in 1998. In July of 1994, a terrorist targeting Argentina's Jewish community detonated a bomb in the AMIA headquarters killing 85 people and injuring hundreds, the deadliest bombing in Argentina history.

In January of 1998, President Bill Clinton was caught in a scandal. He was accused of having "inappropriate relations with a White House intern" (Monica Lewinsky). The U.S. House of Representatives impeached Clinton on December 19, 1998, for perjury under oath, but following an investigation by federal prosecutor Kenneth Starr, the Senate acquitted Clinton on February 12, 1999.

The world of the 1990s had become an increasingly dangerous place, and there were few, if any, safe havens.

It was in this world that Billy became even more introspective. He wanted to inform his wonderful wife, Jen, about his unusual gift, if that is what it was, and he searched for a way he could break the news to her gently. He longed to tell her of the visions of the beautiful little girl of his dreams, the one he first laid eyes on when he was six years of age, the little girl who seemed to age commensurately with him and the one he dreamed he would someday marry. He longed to tell her about dreams about things as mundane as Sandy Amoros's catch, the silliness of seeing D.B. Cooper's hijacking adventure, the chilling assassination of JFK which still haunted him, and he longed to know WHY he was chosen and the identity of who placed these visions in his mind.

After a long discussion with his dear friend Pete Hamill, Billy made a definitive decision to inform his beloved Jen of his unsolved dilemma. He prayed that this information would not dismay the love of his life in any way.

CHAPTER TWENTY-FOUR

Jen's reaction was not entirely unexpected. Upon learning the extensive details of Billy's unusual and improbable bestowal, her eyes welled with tears as it appeared she was attempting to reconcile and fully comprehend and process the information she had been given. At least that was what Billy thought. He was soon to learn a shocking truth. Jen was about to reveal something perhaps even more extraordinary. Something which Jen had kept from Billy since the moment they had met. Jen had lived in fear of this moment for most of her life, but now she had to confront it with the person she loved more than anyone or anything in the world.

Stifling her sobs, Jen spoke.

"I knew you'd find me someday, Billy. Ever since I was six, I knew you'd come looking for me. You see, someone or something, and I'm hoping He's God, also bestowed upon me a gift, or perhaps a curse. When we first met at Madison Square Garden, I had no idea what you'd look like, Billy. I was not given the ability to see the future as you were. I didn't know your name or anything about you. I just knew that you'd come for me eventually."

With that, Jen began sobbing once more and appeared to be disconsolate. As both sat in bed, Billy kissed her and held her before responding.

"It's all right, angel. I'm shaken to the core, but everything will be okay. I love you more than anything in the world, angel."

Billy kissed the tears from Jen's face and swallowed them. Jen attempted to compose herself before replying.

"Billy, I love you with all my heart and soul, but something may not be all right. You see, I knew that if you ever learned the truth about me, that you'd be chosen."

Billy peered at Jen quizzically before responding. He surmised Jen's inference, itself an improbable, however, accurate conclusion. "I really understand, now, sweetheart. All these years, I believed in my heart that this "gift" was merely an exercise in futility and that it would all be in vain. There just had to be an explanation as to why I was provided these visions."

Billy hesitated briefly before continuing. He was almost hesitant to ask. He gulped before asking.

"Jen, do you know what exactly I was chosen for?"

Jen attempted a tearful smile before responding.

"I'm a devout Christian, as I believe you are, too, Billy. It's in your heart. But I really don't know what you've been chosen for, my love. All I knew is that you'd find me and whatever you were chosen for will be something extreme, something ordained."

Jen made the sign of the cross before continuing.

"Although I'm confident that He will guide you, Billy, I'm a bit frightened."

"Frightened of what, Jen?"

"Frightened that I'll lose you."

"You'll never lose me, Jennifer. Just look in your heart, and I'll always be there."

The former Jennifer Swanson smiled bravely and beckoned for Billy to come to her.

"Hold me, Billy."

With that they embraced. They remained in that embrace until morning.

CHAPTER TWENTY-FIVE

"Do you understand, gentlemen, that in all the horror, there is just this: that there is no horror!" – Russian Writer Aleksandr Kuprin

Immediately following Billy's admission and Jen's equally stunning confession, all of Billy's dreams vanished; all that is, except one recurring dream. Despite the fact that Billy had been retired from the FDNY for quite some time, he would endure an intermittent dream in which he entered a large burning building, one filled with smoke so thick that he could hardly see for more than a distance of a few feet. In the recurrent dream, Billy would awake with the feeling that he was desperately searching for specific people, but when he awoke, he could not remember who.

Peter, Billy and Jen's son, was now thirty-two years old and a Federal Agent, a U.S. Marshal. Angela, thirty, who had graduated from Princeton University, was a college professor at her alma mater. Billy, fifty-six, remained fit as did Jen, his still unworldly beautiful and inspirational wife. The twenty-first century had commenced and the world continued to change drastically, and not always for the better. It appeared as if many on the planet had lost their respective souls.

On a bright, sunny September day, Billy awoke, kissed Jen tenderly and prepared to leave for lower Manhattan. He was to attend a meeting of retired Police officers and firefighters. Jen held him particularly tight as they embraced. Jen's grip was tighter than ever before, it was as if she did not want to let go.

On that sunlit morning, Billy arrived at the ballroom where the retired Police and Firefighters had congregated. However, his visit was curtailed when alarms rang out signifying that a major incident had taken place, one that required as much help from Police, Firefighters and emergency EMTs, active or not. Billy, as did many others in attendance, rushed to the scene of the catastrophe. There were already dozens of responders already battling the blaze and all arrivals were given instructions to proceed past the checkpoint at their own peril. Help was desperately needed, but it was made clear that this was a desperate and dangerous situation.

Sirens sounded, and as people ran or were assisted out of the building, only Police, Firefighters and all First Responders ran towards it. Many of the people exiting from the smoky fiery haze had the look of zombies, their eyes vacuous and fearful. They appeared to be in shock, and the look of disbelief and horror was etched on their faces, and they were the lucky ones. As the smoke grew thicker, more ambulances arrived. Many of the people being carried out of the building were on stretchers, and many of them appeared to be lifeless. There just weren't enough emergency personnel on hand to treat them; more EMTs rushed to the scene, brave young men and women not giving thought to the perils of their occupation. There were lives to save.

Billy was one of the First Responders, retirement be damned. Billy rushed into the building as others ran out, folks covered in soot and ash, men and women wanting desperately to return home to their families and loved ones, men and women whose lives would never be the same.

As soon as Billy entered the burning building, the toxic smoke and dirt seared his lungs. Billy, of course, a veteran of many conflagrations, had never experienced any as devastating. The heat he felt was as intense as any he had endured, his eyes seared with unimaginable soreness as he barged into the deadly fray. Firefighters already in the building were shouting that the elevators were not functioning and that a stairwell evacuation was taking place. It was the only way in which to save what was left of the inhabitants of the building which was now engulfed in flames.

As Billy began to climb the stairs in hopes of rescuing those still alive, there were dead bodies strewn throughout the building, incredibly he began to have a distinct and vivid vision. He recalled wondering for much of his life why he had been chosen to see things, events of the future. Suddenly, he instinctively knew that this was his moment. He had been selected to be at this precise location on this fateful day. He recalled beautiful Jen's words, "Whatever you've been chosen for will be something extreme, something ordained."

It was at that exact moment that Billy began experiencing a vivid Epiphany. It was clear as day, his dreams and visions were now entering his mind fast and furiously. He **KNEW** where to look in order to be the savior for whom he was designated.

"Quick," he thought, "behind the third floor staircase."

She was there, just as Billy's vision had guided him. But there was a reason! Billy knew it wasn't the Haitian woman he was saving. It was her unborn granddaughter, a woman who would not be born for forty years, a woman who would go on to cure Alzheimer's and Dementia.

The woman choked as Billy carried her down the staircase and out into the street. As he handed her to the EMTs, she called out softly to him, "God bless you!"

But Billy was not done. His visions were coming rapidly. The vision directed him to a fourth floor office in order to save a young Jamaican man named Desmond. Billy **KNEW** that he'd be trapped beneath a massive file cabinet, gasping for air. As Billy attempted to rescue the entrapped man from below the metal storage case, huge burning debris fell from above, just inches from where he struggled to free the victim. Summoning strength he never even imagined he had, Billy somehow extricated the helpless man from the rubble. The heroic act was witnessed by two other firefighters who watched in amazement and awe at both Billy's improbable strength and bravery. One of the firefighters remarked to the other, "How the hell did he do that?! It's as if he's possessed by the devil!" The other firefighter responded, "If he's possessed, it's by the man upstairs, not the devil!" Billy knew that it was not only the Jamaican man he was saving, but his unborn son, a man who would become a renowned cardiologist.

Billy once more raced into the burning building and ran up the stairs to the fifth floor. Many other firefighters were receiving oxygen in front of the building which had become an inferno, but Billy knew why he had to rush back in. Billy **KNEW** that the man whose life he was saving would have a son who would go on to win a Nobel Peace prize in Medicine. Billy, choking, reached the man at exactly the spot he saw in his vision. However, he knew that his job had not yet ended.

Billy rushed in and raced to the second floor. The young Russian Jewish woman was literally lying face down on the ground. She was rapidly losing consciousness and Billy **KNEW** exactly where he'd find her. He also **KNEW** she would have a grandson who would go on to save dozens of her patients suffering from chronic illnesses as a physician at New York's Sloan Kettering Cancer Institute. Billy gathered her up and raced down the staircase, carrying her to salvation.

Billy was not done, however. He **KNEW** where to find a Rabbi who was visiting a friend on the sixth floor of the building, a young Rabbi who would go on to tutor several youngsters in Israel, many of whom would make significant contributions to society.

Billy was on a mission. Time and time again, he would brave the odds and rescue folks, all with families to go home to, all with promising futures. There were teachers, attorneys, mechanics, librarians and on and on. Billy would literally SEE their families as they returned home to their loved ones, and see them as they entered the homes of those waiting anxiously to see if their husbands, wives, brothers and sisters had survived, and Billy would see them BEFORE he rescued each individual.

Billy rushed back in to save an Islamic woman, a woman in her twenties, a woman whose unborn daughter would go on to become a renowned heart surgeon and save countless lives. He **KNEW** where to find her. She was in the kitchen in her second floor office, hiding behind a closed door, fearful to move. Billy found her at precise the location his vision guided him to. He carried her in his arms out into the street where he handed her to the EMTs.

The EMTs attempted to convince Billy not to reenter the building, which seemed to be engulfed in flames. They sensed accurately that Billy was in dire straits and he too required serious medical attention. However, their efforts to restrain him failed, and Billy rushed back into the inferno. He **KNEW** that he must race back to the fifth floor where he was certain he would find a young pregnant woman who would later give birth to a son, a scientist who would go on to cure Crohn's and Colitis, two previously incurable, insidious diseases. Billy located her where he had envisioned as she lay under a desk, gasping and choking for breath. Billy scooped her up and with all the strength he had left in his failing body, he ran down the treacherous stairs, through a thickening cloud of smoke and onto the street. The young woman was then taken by the EMTS and moments later Billy crumpled to the pavement. He had fulfilled his purpose.

Minutes later, there was a huge booming sound. The building had begun to collapse.

As Billy breathed his last, thoughts feverishly entered his mind. He actually managed a smile as he envisioned Sandy Amoros racing into the left field corner